# 100 Word Horrors

# Presented by

# Kevin J. Kennedy

100 Word Horrors © 2018 Kevin J. Kennedy

Compiled by Kevin J. Kennedy

Edited by Brandy Yassa

Cover design by Michael Bray

Each story in this book has been published with the authors' permission. They are all copyrighted by the author. All rights reserved. No part of this publication may be reproduced, distributed, or transmitted in any form or by any means, including photocopying, recording, or other electronic or mechanical methods, without the prior written permission of the publisher, except in the case of brief quotations embodied in critical reviews and certain other non-commercial uses permitted by copyright law.

First Printing, 2018

## Acknowledgements

I would firstly like to thank Brandy Yassa. Brandy is the editor of everything published by KJK Publishing and without her I would probably still be spending most of my time sending stories into other peoples books, rather than putting them together. She does an amazing job and is a pleasure to work with. We have worked on four anthologies together and one novella, so far, and I can only hope that we will work on many more projects in the years to come.

I'd also like to thank every author that has worked with me so far. I'm very early in my career and it means a lot to me that authors trust me with their work. I only hope that I can continue to publish books that make the authors proud to be a part of what I'm doing.

Thanks to Michael Bray for an amazing cover and Ronald Malfi, for providing the cover blurb.

Thanks to my mother and father for everything.

Most importantly, thanks to everyone who has picked up a copy of the book. Without you, none of us would be doing this. Writing stories is a pointless endeavour if no one reads them. You give us the opportunity to try and be who we want to be, and for that I can't thank you enough.

Kevin J. Kennedy

## Table of Contents

Foreword ............................................................................................................................. 9

The Dead Thing By Lisa Morton ...................................................................................... 11

Hide and Seek By Matthew Brockmeyer ....................................................................... 12

They Came for Me By Glenn Rolfe ................................................................................. 13

Lunchtime By Andrew Lennon ....................................................................................... 14

Strength in the Blood By A.J. Brown .............................................................................. 15

It is Just Local Gossip By Norbert Gora .......................................................................... 16

Just A Game By Christopher Motz .................................................................................. 17

Firing Squad By Mark Fleming ........................................................................................ 18

Alone By Brandy Yassa .................................................................................................... 19

Baby Steps By Michael A. Arnzen ................................................................................... 20

A Song For Them By Mark Cassell .................................................................................. 21

The Other Me By P.J. Blakey-Novis ................................................................................ 22

Late Night Drive By John Dover ...................................................................................... 23

Hobby By Matt Hickman ................................................................................................. 24

Beauty Mask By Sara Tantlinger ..................................................................................... 25

Bessy By Mark Lumby ..................................................................................................... 26

Heart Shaped Box By Pippa Bailey ................................................................................. 27

Post Halloween By Veronica Smith ................................................................................ 28

The Man in the Black Sweater By Richard Chizmar ...................................................... 29

Virtual Reality By David Owain Hughes ......................................................................... 30

I Was Loved By P.J. Blakey-Novis ................................................................................... 31

| | |
|---|---|
| The End of the Pier By Amy Cross | 32 |
| The Dublin Pub By Veronica Smith | 33 |
| I Am The End By Michael Bray | 34 |
| Beasts from Below By Alex Laybourne | 35 |
| Coming Home By Suzanne Fox | 36 |
| Stone Dry By Sara Tantlinger | 37 |
| The Box By Valerie Lioudis | 38 |
| Best of Friends By Stefan Lear | 39 |
| It Came By Mark Lumby | 40 |
| Cold Toes By Georgia Lennon | 41 |
| Edmond By James Matthew Buyers | 42 |
| Knock Knock.. By C.S Anderson | 43 |
| Delusional By Suzanne Fox | 44 |
| Disregarded Advice By Ike Hamill | 45 |
| Harsh Sentence By P. Mattern | 46 |
| No More By Mike Duke | 47 |
| What is Schizophrenia, Anyway? By Robert W. Easton | 48 |
| Shower Thoughts By Peter Oliver Wonder | 49 |
| A Caring Community? By Suzanne Fox | 50 |
| Lightbulb By Matthew Brockmeyer | 51 |
| A Demonic Pact By Billy San Juan | 52 |
| Till Death do us Part By Derek Shupert | 53 |
| Someone's in my House By Gord Rollo | 54 |
| It By Billy Chizmar | 55 |
| Checkmate Roommate By Michael A. Arnzen | 56 |
| Silence By Pippa Bailey | 57 |
| Jolly Ol' Infiltrator By Weston Kincade | 58 |

Shadows By Antonio Simon, Jr. ........................................................................................................... 59

Winter's Embrace By Duncan P. Bradshaw .......................................................................................... 60

Cut Down to Size By David Owain Hughes .......................................................................................... 61

Children of the Carnival By Kevin J. Kennedy ..................................................................................... 62

The Grave By Amy Cross ..................................................................................................................... 63

Will-o'-the-Wisp By Nicholas Diak ...................................................................................................... 64

Stone By Becky Narron ........................................................................................................................ 65

Meal for One By Howard Carlyle ......................................................................................................... 66

Don't Look Back By James Matthew Buyers ....................................................................................... 67

Street-Hearts By Chris Kelso ................................................................................................................ 68

Consumed by Desire By Adriaan Brae ................................................................................................. 69

Another Tonight? By William F. Nolan ................................................................................................ 70

Destiny's Embrace By Michael Paul Gonzalez ..................................................................................... 71

Clean By Valerie Lioudis ...................................................................................................................... 72

Trees By Donelle Pardee Whiting ........................................................................................................ 73

Dancing By David Owain Hughes ........................................................................................................ 74

Running from Him By Michael A. Arnzen ........................................................................................... 75

Night Terrors By Lisa Vasquez ............................................................................................................. 76

It's Just a Dream, Right? By Ellen A. Easton ........................................................................................ 77

Over the Edge By Mark Cassell ........................................................................................................... 78

The Beauty of the Sea By Kevin J. Kennedy ........................................................................................ 79

Breadth of Bone By Sara Tantlinger .................................................................................................... 80

Never Leave Me, Nor Forsake Me By Mike Duke ............................................................................... 81

Escape By Megan Ince ......................................................................................................................... 82

Forever Men By Eric J. Guignard .......................................................................................................... 83

The Artist By Howard Carlyle ............................................................................................................... 84

Initiation By Mark Fleming .................................................................................................................. 85

| | |
|---|---|
| What's For Dinner? By Christopher Motz | 86 |
| Vermillion By Lisa Vasquez | 87 |
| Jack Frost By Christina Bergling | 88 |
| Coming Around By C.M. Saunders | 89 |
| Bad Cop, Bad Cop By James H Longmore | 90 |
| Experimental Animal 7 By Lee McGeorge | 91 |
| Bummed Light By James Matthew Byers | 92 |
| Sugar & Spice By Chad Lutzke | 93 |
| Air By Dave McClusky | 94 |
| You Don't See Me By Christina Bergling | 95 |
| The Dead Train By Craig Saunders | 96 |
| Delivery By Briana Robertson | 97 |
| The Guest By Dave McCluskey | 98 |
| Nights in Whitechapel By Theresa Jacobs | 99 |
| Betrayal By Lee Mountford | 100 |
| Beautiful Francesca By Ike Hamill | 101 |
| Priscilla's Pugnacious Pampered Pups By Brandy Yassa | 102 |
| Mister Fancy Pants By Rhys Hughes | 103 |
| Greed Has No Heart By Mark Lumby | 104 |
| Beast in the Bedroom By Pippa Bailey | 105 |
| The Boy By Richard Chizmar and Billy Chizmar | 106 |
| Weeping Keys By Elizabeth Cash | 107 |
| Grand Slam By Christina Bergling | 108 |
| Shock Collar By Jeff Strand | 109 |
| The Festival of Gluttony By Mike Duke | 110 |
| Selfie By Rick Gualtieri | 111 |
| Jonathan By Amy Cross | 112 |

A Flash Beginning By Jessica Gomez .................................................................................................... 113

Spellbound By John Dover ...................................................................................................................... 114

I Was a Teenage Eulogist By Jason M. Light............................................................................................. 115

From the Mouths of Drunks and Babes By Alex Laybourne .................................................................... 116

Stage Fright By James McCulloch............................................................................................................ 117

Cupid and Death By Rhys Hughes ........................................................................................................... 118

The Feast By Rebecca Brae ..................................................................................................................... 119

The Dolls By Mark Lukens ....................................................................................................................... 120

Afterword................................................................................................................................................ 121

Also available on Amazon from KJK Publishing ...................................................................................... 122

## Foreword

When I started writing, I was always looking for anthologies that were taking really short stories, as I didn't have a lot of faith in my writing. I was working on the basis that if the stories were short I could write more, heightening my chances of getting accepted. What I later realised was that it was much harder to tell a full story in a really short piece of flash fiction. I noticed that every story that I wrote was becoming longer and longer, as I had bigger stories to tell and more I wanted to say in them, but I had already developed a love for flash fiction and had read some really good stories along the way. I had also come across 'drabbles.' A drabble is a story of exactly one hundred words, not including the title. Drabbles can be a lot of fun to write, but can also have you pulling your hair out. Every time you add a line, you need to take another out. As you write it you always think of things to add, but each word is so precious that the drabbles go through more re-writes than most longer stories ever will.

I liked the idea of putting a book of drabbles together, but I knew I would need a lot of stories. I had no idea how many authors would be interested in writing a drabble, so I decided to ask them. The response was overwhelming and the drabbles started flooding in almost instantly.

Submissions to the book were almost entirely invite only and I opened it to a few small groups. I received hundreds of drabbles. The book you hold in your hands contains the best in my opinion and each drabble is a complete little contained story.

As always with my anthologies, you will find Bram Stoker award winners, Amazon top sellers, the best indie writers and a few newer writers, who just hit the nail on the head with their stories.

Some people will read the book cover to cover and others will use it as a table top book and read a drabble or two a day. Whatever you do, I encourage you to take a minute after you read each drabble, and have a think about it. There is a lot packed into each of these little one hundred word stories. I only hope you enjoy reading them as much as I did.

Kevin J. Kennedy

"I didn't have time to write a short letter, so I wrote a long one instead."

— Mark Twain

## The Dead Thing

## By

## Lisa Morton

I'm watching the dead thing in the corner when it moves.

It's a big black mass, tall, like Mama, with the rough shape of a body, a head, and legs. I've been watching it since we came here, but this is the first time it's moved.

Mama doesn't see it. Or can't. She just keeps sitting in the chair not far away, watching me instead of it.

"What are you looking at?"

It hovers away from the wall.

It floats toward Mama.

And then it goes into Mama.

"Come here, you stupid cat," she says as she reaches for me.

## Hide and Seek

## By

## Matthew Brockmeyer

There was nothing I loved more than playing hide and seek at the dump with my friends on warm summer evenings. And I was always the best at it. Searching out the most imaginative places to hide amongst the piles of trash and rows of wrecked cars, and remain so still and quiet. Like the time I squeezed into that dirty, old-fashioned refrigerator.

*They'll never find me here*, I thought, pulling the door shut and hearing the lock click shut.

And they never did.

Never found me, no matter how hard I pounded against the door and screamed for help.

## They Came for Me

## By

## Glenn Rolfe

The spiders crawled through the bedroom window. Ice spilled down my spine as I clenched the sheets over my nose, hiding, but unable to look away. They chose Billy first. An avalanche of arachnids the size of baseballs spilled through the broken screen and flowed to my older brother's bed as if carried on the sea. Up they went, thousands of legs. They covered every inch of his exposed body, and then stopped. One climbed over the rest and disappeared into Billy's mouth. All at once, his body jolted, and then lay still.

I screamed.

Then they came for me.

# Lunchtime

## By

## Andrew Lennon

Alex mixed his minced meat into his mashed potato, the moistness of the gravy created a slurping sound as the fork pushed and pulled through the meal. Alex continued to stir, waiting for the meal to cool enough to be able to eat, the smell of pepper filling his nose.

Jonny entered the office. "Oh, that smells good, mate. What are you eating today?"

"Cottage pie," Alex replied.

"Nice, not had that in ages."

"Do you want some?" Alex asked.

Jonny took a bite and savoured the flavour. "Hey, where's Anne?"

Alex smiled and raised the plate to offer more.

## Strength in the Blood

## By

## A.J. Brown

I knelt in the kitchen, hands folded in prayer.

"You gave me strength."

Eyes open, I stared. *I cleaned up my wife's blood there.*

"You gave me strength," I repeated in the den. *I cleaned Paul's blood from the carpet.*

"You gave me strength."

In the bathroom, *I washed Kerri's blood off the walls.*

In the baby's room, I closed my eyes against tears.

"Give me strength."

Red stains soaked the crib where Charlotte once slept.

In the half bathroom I stared at my reflection. A shadow grinned back, it's eyes red.

"I am strength," it said. And it laughed.

## It is Just Local Gossip

### By

### Norbert Gora

I came to this backwater where (or because) the inhabitants swore that there was a miracle at the local cemetery.

On a starry night, a dead man would appear at his tombstone.

What fool would believe it?

Camera clenched firmly in hand, I boldly crossed the graveyard boundary.

As expected, there was nothing to see, but emptiness.

Before a curse word could leave my lips, I felt an agonizing chill upon my neck.

"It's just local gossip. Dead men don't leave their coffins," a cold voice suddenly whispered behind my back.

I didn't have to turn around to know it was over.

## Just A Game

## By

## Christopher Motz

Jack gave each of his four friends a small, clear capsule and took his place in the circle.

"How does this game work?" Jenna asked.

"You all wait and see who can last the longest," he replied.

"But if we're all going to be trippin', who's going to be keeping time?" Mary asked.

"I will," Jack replied.

"This is stupid," Brian laughed. "Who ever heard of a game where the point is to stay high the longest?"

"Well that's the fun part," Jack smiled. "I didn't give you acid."

"Oh, it's Ecstasy," Jason shouted happily.

"Nope," Jack laughed, "it's cyanide."

## Firing Squad

## By

## Mark Fleming

Tyrone was spray-painting the railway tunnel. Shoogling the near-empty tin, he noticed something poking from the shale. He clawed at it. It was a wallet, the contents remarkably preserved, including a faded photograph of a kilted soldier. Apparently a troop train crashed here years before; volunteers en route to the Western Front. Ditching the wallet, he absently fired a jet over it until just the soldier's eyes were exposed, glaring vengefully from the luminous goo. Now his legs had turned to jelly. The fumes were overpowering him. He felt faint. He could hardly feel the vibration of the oncoming train.

## Alone

## By

## Brandy Yassa

It was a simple test, they said. Nothing to it.

"We'll be with you all the way," they said.

So, they prepped me, then placed me into a very narrow, long tube… and left me.

The magnets began their banging, so horribly loud, even with my earplugs.

Through a speaker they spoke, reassuring me all was well.

The magnets resumed their infernal banging, banging so loudly, I whimpered.

They heard. "How're you doing?" they asked.

Without waiting, they continued, "Just a little longer, nothing to worry about."

A jovial voice added, "Just bear with us."

Then, the lights went out.

## Baby Steps

## By

## Michael A. Arnzen

Teaching my toddling son to walk is exhausting us both. We're red-faced, hostile. Holding his fat little hand as he lumbers up from a crawl, I hoist him so high his arm might pop out from the socket like a doll's. But this time he magically catches his balance, swings out a leg and lurches forward like a dinosaur, erect. He swivels his hips and lands the next step solid. This time, he didn't trip over his tail. He balances above the volcano's edge, high on his hooves. He smiles up at his daddy, and then surveys his future dominion.

## A Song For Them

## By

## Mark Cassell

The woodwind melody drifted from their cabin and she pictured Neil still hunched, the flute at his lips. Overshadowed by the boat, Ronette knelt on the jetty. She gripped weathered planks to gaze into the water. A bitterness clogged her throat, tears cooling her cheeks.

Something stirred the depths, rising: pale face, dead eyes bulging amid puffy flesh. It broke the surface with a cloying stink of fish and rot.

The euphonious tune continued.

A bloated hand burst upwards in a rush of salty water.

The melody played on the breeze. Cold fingers clamped her wrist.

Ronette began to sing.

## The Other Me

## By

## P.J. Blakey-Novis

It is difficult to describe what it looks like, always in the periphery of my vision. Occasionally I catch a glimpse of the white eyes, the blackened teeth. If I try to focus on it, then it disappears. Paranoia personified. Following me. Always close, yet out of reach. It is dangerous, claiming victims wherever I go, leaving them for me to find. I'm always the one who finds the bodies; they are my hands which turn crimson under the moonlight. One day it will take me too, but only when it is ready. For now, I wait, avoiding the shadows.

## Late Night Drive

## By

## John Dover

Thump, thump, thump

My tires bounce across the center lane, jostling me awake. My eyes itch and burn from staring too long, the eyelids chafe my iris, straining with raw effort to stay closed, but I fight them open. Heavy, inky rain hisses underneath and my engine roars. The chains hooked to my bumper hammer away with their syncopated song. A rush of wind and I finally hear my passenger tear loose from his bonds, rolling broken, limp, and probably dead. I am free of the bastard. He shouldn't have let his dog shit on my lawn.

Thump, thump, thump.

# Hobby

## By

## Matt Hickman

The bellicose, coppery aroma of spilled blood, interspersed with the putrid stench of his voided bowels hangs in the air.

I breathe it in, and revel in his suffering. His ruined carcass lays slumped in the chair in a defeated posture. A stream of warm claret dribbles from his fingertips to the wooden, blood soaked floorboards.

I hear a familiar voice, calling from a distance.

*Damn.*

I dance across the room in elation, carefully shut and lock the door of my treehouse, and begin to descend the rickety, wooden ladder.

"Coming, mom."

*I wonder what's for dinner. Hope its spaghetti.*

## Beauty Mask

## By

## Sara Tantlinger

*Step 1: Exfoliate*, stated the bottle clutched in Remy's hand. She lathered her face with the gunk and tiny beads slathered off dead skin cells. The scent claimed to be blood-orange, but a sour, metallic odor exploded from the beads the more she rubbed them. *After exfoliating, rinse and place the beauty mask over your face for 15 minutes*. Remy tore off the plastic and pulled the package out, delighted that the mask was fresher than the last one she bought. The tone matched her skin much better, plus there were fewer maggots clinging from the flesh covering the eyeholes.

# Bessy

## By

## Mark Lumby

A watchman for forty-five years.

I waited until the manager left, let myself in.

"I'm not ready to go," I told myself. "I'm not leaving you, Bessy."

I stepped up to her, running a hand over her cold metal, her cutting blade shining suggestively.

I climbed inside her, feet first and stomach against her surface. I took a last look around before flicking the switch.

The clamp shattered my spine; my stomach exploded. The blade released, waist separating away from my torso. I was alive when my blood warmed my death bed.

"I'll not leave you, Bessy," I murmured.

## Heart Shaped Box

## By

## Pippa Bailey

My naked body quivered, legs splayed on the hospital bed. The stink of bleach and decay stung my nostrils, and marred my tongue. A masked doctor slid the lower scissor blade into me –slicing. He split me from pelvis to neck. A jagged wound of effluence. My heart, no longer of use, was torn from its resting place.

His fingers caressed a golden box of puzzle and sin. It spewed forth a slick, undulating black which filled the aching void, that was my broken heart. Replaced with a darkness that consumed all thought, all feeling, and would know no bounds.

## Post Halloween

## By

## Veronica Smith

Halloween was over, but Kim was reluctant to take down her decorations. She loved Halloween, her favorite season. She sighed and pulled a moaning ghost down. As she dropped it into the storage bin, it flew up and went right back to where it was before, laughing. She whirled around at the sound of all her decorations laughing. Normally she loved them but now they were scaring her. Suddenly she felt her body folding and being forced into the bin.

As the lid was locked down over her she heard, "That will be the last time she puts us away!"

## The Man in the Black Sweater

### By

## Richard Chizmar

The beer was gone. The fire was dying. A chill had crept into the autumn night air.

"What's the worst thing you've ever done?"

The boy in the red hat spoke up first. He was drunk.

"I killed someone once. A hit and run. I was speeding and it was an accident, but I could have maybe saved the girl's life if I had called for help. Instead I got back into my car and left her there."

The man in the black sweater slid the knife out of his pants pocket. After three long years, he had found him.

## Virtual Reality

## By

## David Owain Hughes

Danny's hands ripped at the bright birthday paper like a zombie at flesh.

"Hell, yeah, *King Kong*," his pre-pubescent voice cracked.

He lifted the flap on his VR system, slid the game in and hit play. His TV exploded to life with colour and sound, a gorilla roared, beating its chest.

"This is going to be *killer*—"

The television turned off, the console's door flew open, and the game was spat out, hitting Danny in the face. The boy's eyes widened when a huge, flaming barrel squeezed out of his machine and hurtled towards him.

"*Fuck*. This is—"

## I Was Loved

### By

### P.J. Blakey-Novis

I died for her. Not in some heroic way, but because it was what she wanted. Death changes your perspective, in the most literal way, as I look down on my still-warm corpse, watching her scrape the rest of the poisoned meal into the bin. I promised I'd do anything for her, so I pretended not to know she was killing me, slowly, for months. It didn't hurt, and it made her happy. Therefore, I have no complaints, no interest in knowing her reasons. She loved me, she owned me, and finally she set me free. My mistress, my wife.

## The End of the Pier

## By

## Amy Cross

When you think about chaining a concrete block to your leg and jumping off the end of the pier, you probably imagine sinking into a glittering blue sea and falling serenely to the bottom, but it's not like that at all. The truth is you're immediately swallowed by dirty, ice-cold darkness and you start panicking. You sink deeper and deeper until you hit the bottom, and there you start gulping great mouthfuls of filthy sediment. It's so dark as you're buried alive in the water. And then, as you die, you start wondering where all the hands are coming from.

## The Dublin Pub

## By

## Veronica Smith

The Dublin Pub was quiet when Anthony walked in the open door. He was to meet some friends for a drink. Stepping inside, he saw that it was empty, not a soul around. The neon sign behind the bar flickered in the darkness. He leaned over the bar and saw several bodies. Hearing the fluttering of wings near the rafters, he looked up. To his horror, his friends were hanging there, but not by their necks.

They were hanging like bats, their faces and chests were covered in blood. He didn't even get to scream when they dropped on him.

## I Am The End

## By

## Michael Bray

I am the whisper in the wind, the goosebumps on your skin.

I am the cold spot in the corner of this shadow draped room.

I am the black, the endless night.

I watch you sleep your untroubled dreams, each breath the only sound in this old house.

I touch your cheek, causing you to stir as I whisper into your ear.

This is your last, the end.

No time left to achieve those hopes and dreams.

I kiss your lips, stealing that last delicious breath as the house falls silent.

You belong to me now, forever by my side.

## Beasts from Below

### By

### Alex Laybourne

Nobody knew where they came from. All they knew was that one night they went to bed, and by the morning, the monsters had arrived. They had never seen anything like it before.

Rising up from under the earth, the woken giants wasted no time in claiming back their land. They slaughtered humans by the dozens, sweeping through towns like a plague. They killed for pleasure, leaving bodies to rot where they fell.

But the fight was far from over. The new commander smiled, as he pressed the button that launched the nukes, and started what he called 'mankind's revenge'.

## Coming Home

## By

## Suzanne Fox

Excitement and elation quivered through Dexter with the intensity of an electrical current. He had conquered the odds and was ready to quash the critics who had dismissed his genius as folly.

The hum of the time machine faded as he returned from a forthcoming century to his own. Dexter stepped out, disease-free, and improved to perfection after his encounter with future humanity.

His welcoming committee screamed. The barrel of a gun raised. He turned, catching sight of a monster reflected in the window. An exposed brain protected by a glass dome, a metallic breast plate, and Dexter's confused eyes.

## Stone Dry

## By

## Sara Tantlinger

"We gotta do something about Momma," Billy said, his throat as dry as the fields. "She doesn't want me here." Momma didn't understand his relationship with Ash.

Ash said nothing, just stared with that gray glare.

"Momma ain't been right since the baby. Pa says she brought the drought, like a witch. You know they used to burn witches? Or maybe stone them..."

Billy nodded. "You're right. I don't want Momma to suffer." His hand wrapped around Ash's weight. The dark, pointed stone brought warmth onto his palm. Billy clutched the jagged rock and headed home to end the drought.

## The Box

## By

## Valerie Lioudis

Gasp. Struggling, I try to pull enough air in to keep myself from passing out. Gasp. It isn't working. The box feels like it's closing in on me. Blood falls from my finger onto my face as I attempt to claw my way through the pine box. Gasp. The spinning has begun. Fireflies explode in my eyes. Gasp. Molten lava fills my lungs with scorching hot pain. The rhythmic thump of each shovel load of dirt lulls me to sleep. Gasp. Last one. Thrashing, I fight against death, but death wrestles me down, and the shovel empties again.

## Best of Friends

## By

## Stefan Lear

I'm a people person. I value the bonds, the memories, I create with another person. I'm not into superficial friendships, though. I want to explore relationships that will last a lifetime. I want to know you inside and out. I'll do whatever it takes to completely and utterly understand my friends. It's my belief that you never really know someone until you've looked someone in the eye as they beg for their life. "I'm sorry," were the last words whimpered with his final breath. His eyes faded dull and all life left his body. I am not a superficial friend.

## It Came

## By

## Mark Lumby

They watched it from the bridge, tall and shadowed from the river side, loose skin moving from maggots underneath.

I stood trembling from behind, couldn't see what it was doing as people from the bridge screamed warnings. Some were silent in horror. Some were vomiting.

It was ten feet tall, head hunched into its wide shoulders like it was decapitated.

I shuffled through the leaves, catching its attention, its dark eyes shimmering.

But it didn't care.

I moved closer. I could smell it: decay and fish. Blood poured onto the grass as it took another bite from the dog's stomach.

## Cold Toes

## By

## Georgia Lennon

I swear if his cold toes touch me one more time, I'll bury him; they're like little ice cubes for Christ's sake and it's only November. At least I don't have to worry about him stealing the covers, he costs a fortune in heating bills. Maybe I'll try soaking them in boiling water this time, see if that'll warm 'em up? Attempting to shove him into the oven last night wasn't the brightest of ideas I'll admit, but what do you expect? I miss his warmth. If he hadn't tried to leave me, then perhaps he would still be alive.

# Edmond

## By

## James Matthew Buyers

There may be better ways to die

Than buried to the neck,

And all the dust here in my eyes

As ravens stoop to peck

Reminding me I had to pay

To find myself in dirt.

The witch had said, "Come have your way."

And no, it didn't hurt

Until she bared her dripping fangs

And nicked me on my chin,

Unleashing all her hunger pangs,

A fearful, haunting grin.

She took my essence, aging me,

But that was quite alright.

The ants all down below the tree

Enjoy each tiny bite.

Her spell,

My hell

To dwell.

Goodnight ..

## Knock Knock..

## By

## C.S Anderson

They were at the fucking door.

They had found her.

Again.

Shit.

She was sure she had masked her path to this place, scrubbed it squeaky damn clean, as a matter of fact, but she must have screwed up somewhere because here they were.

Knocking at her damn door.

Crap.

She took a moment to consider her options.

It didn't take long.

They all sucked.

Which just meant picking the one that sucked the least.

Which also sucked.

Moving gingerly to the door, she undid the security chain with shaking hands.

"Trump Supporters!" they chirp at her.

God help her…

# Delusional

## By

## Suzanne Fox

"You're not real."

"But, you can see me."

"The doctor says that you're a hallucination. You only exist in my mind."

"You know that's not true."

"You're not real! Not rea... Argh!"

"Tell me that the blood dripping from your wrist isn't real and that I didn't cut you." The demonic figure licked the red gore from its claw and retreated to the corner of the room. Neil screamed.

The lock clacked, and the door opened. "Doctor!" yelled the white-clad nurse, rushing to apply pressure to the wound. "How do you manage to self-harm, when you're cuffed to the bed?"

## Disregarded Advice

## By

## Ike Hamill

BANG!

He cowers under the blankets, holding his breath, knowing that...

BANG! BANG!

...two more will come.

A few days ago, when the pounding first came, he convinced himself that it was only a vivid dream. Two nights ago, he blamed the wind and spent the next day securing the shutters on the north side of the house.

When he was a boy, his mother warned him.

"The third time it comes, don't be home."

For two days, he could have been on the road, getting far away.

"It will come for blood," she said.

He hears the doorknob click.

# Harsh Sentence

## By

## P. Mattern

The philanderer felt a sharp blow to the back of his ankles and was immediately awake, warm blood enveloping his bare feet.

Violet was standing several feet away from their bed, still in her nightgown, a dripping axe in her hand.

He arose and pitched helplessly forward, much like the character in his last novel had, and instantly recognized that she had severed his Achilles tendon.

She'd always been big on poetic justice.

"Why?" he grunted, realizing as he spoke that it was the most useless question he could ask.

Her only answer was a final blow to his head.

## No More

## By

## Mike Duke

Bruised eye, swollen shut. Broken jaw, broken orbit, broken arm.

"Fell down the stairs again, doc. Such a klutz, I know. Fourth time this year. Worst one yet, and, dammit, it was on Christmas Day. Yeah. It *did* ruin things for the kids. My fault. *ALL* my fault. As usual."

But tonight, he hit my son.

New Year's Eve. The ball's about to drop. I stand behind my husband's favorite chair, where, drunk, he sleeps. Cheers on TV. A new year. A new day. Double-barrel shotgun in hand, I resolve...*NO MORE*.

Two triggers at once and I'm free. Free, indeed.

# What is Schizophrenia, Anyway?

## By

## Robert W. Easton

A year ago, I started to hear things. Screaming, crying, begging, growling, and the tearing of flesh. My psychologist gave me a prescription, which kept the sounds at bay.

I came home early from a party, as I could feel the blockers wearing off. The initial terror in the voices had faded, but I was still on the meds. There was a light on in my kitchen, and as I entered the house, the light clicked off. I heard a low growl just before the voice in my head said, "Noooo, this is how I died!" It was my voice.

## Shower Thoughts

### By

## Peter Oliver Wonder

Shutting off the shower, Jane relaxed and inhaled a deep breath of steam. For a moment, she rested against the metal handle and allowed the water to drip from her face—she blew away the drop of water that had accumulated at the bottom of her upper lip.

As she let the warmth embrace her, she was jolted by the thunderous sound which boomed from beside her. Sliding open the shattered glass door, she was surprised to find her three-year-old son standing there with his father's service revolver.

"I'm sorry, mommy," he said before watching her fall to her knees.

## A Caring Community?

## By

## Suzanne Fox

Every day Kitty stood by the roadside cursing, throwing stones at passing cars, and scrabbling for discarded dog-ends to feed her nicotine addiction. A figure of ridicule for the neighbour's kids, who dared each other to knock on her door.

Then, one day, Kitty wasn't there; or the following days.

Two boys dared each other to enter the darkness of her derelict home. Her tortured corpse awaited their discovery in the bedroom, clouded by five weeks of decay. No one had missed her. No one had heard her screams of anguish, or the laughter of her tormentors as she died.

## Lightbulb

### By

## Matthew Brockmeyer

I'm trying to watch the Raiders game but my wife keeps nagging me to go down to the basement and change the lightbulb.

It's first and ten on the twenty-two yard line with a minute left, and she's standing in front of the television in a dirty nightgown, hair a mess, wagging a finger at me, harping about how dark it is down there.

"Yeah, yeah," I say, trying to peer around her, "I'll get to it."

But there's no way I'm going down there. I haven't been down in the basement since I buried her nagging-ass there years ago.

## A Demonic Pact

## By

## Billy San Juan

There's a demon in my bedroom. It follows me with its fiery eyes, daring me to escape. I tried to run already, but he roared, and I fell. My arm landed on the corner of the dresser. I can already feel the bruise forming. It knows the bruise hurts. It knows to grab me by the arm, to squeeze the bruise. To cover my mouth with his clawed talon so I can't scream. I've been trapped with this demon before, but I can usually escape. Not tonight. Tonight, I think I will die. I can't believe I married this man.

## Till Death do us Part

## By

## Derek Shupert

Travis leaned against the door, his vision blurry from the tears that filled his eyes. He had a nasty gash on the right side of his face. Blood dripped from the open wound to the cream-colored linoleum floor. His white shirt was stained red all over.

He slowly twisted his wedding band around his finger. The banging on the door continued to rattle his nerves. Simple grunts and growls mixed in with scratching along the door's wooden exterior. Wiping the tears away, Travis grabbed his ax and got to his feet.

"Till death do us part, my beloved," he muttered.

## Someone's in my House

## By

## Gord Rollo

Someone's in my house.

They're being quiet, but I can still hear them.

Coming upstairs.

I think I know who; the man in the leather jacket I caught peeking in my window earlier today, his skin a sickly shade of alabaster. He said he was an old friend, and something in his jaundiced eyes demanded I let him in. No chance of that. The police assured me he was long gone, but obviously they were wrong. He's back now... just outside my room.

The door swings open.

An old friend?

The knife in the big man's hand tells me no.

# It

## By

## Billy Chizmar

"Ground Control, this is Robinson, I have landed, I repeat, I have touched down."

Robinson's radio exploded with cheers. He was the lone astronaut on the first privately funded mission to the moon, in a rocket that he'd helped design. As he stepped out of the lunar lander, he couldn't help but think about how wealthy he would be by the end of the...

He saw It then. It was moving through the abyss of space as if It were water. Robinson watched as the being moved upon Earth, and with an impossible maw, devoured the planet in one motion.

## Checkmate Roommate

## By

## Michael A. Arnzen

They tormented him just for wearing his chess team t-shirt freshman year, so he dropped out and got a shitty job laying tile. Part of him was too smart for it, but he still got richer and stronger than they ever would, and it gave him time to plan.

Now he had enough tiles to enjoy his own bathroom floor. An ivory checkerboard pattern of chipped skull. He kept their tiny bones, a phalanx of knights and pawns, within his vanity mirror. Alone, he'd practice gambits against himself for days. Despite losing mate after mate, both sides were always victorious.

## Silence

## By

## Pippa Bailey

Jerry liked the silence. His neighbours, despite repeat requests, refused to quieten down, blaring shit music at all hours. No matter how often he complained, the police were uninterested in his plight.

His neighbours didn't hear him enter through the shutter door that night. Nor his footsteps on the wooden floor, creaks hidden beneath thumping drum and bass

Blood trickled from his head, and stained his crisp, white shirt. The rusty screwdriver he had thrust into his ears brought the sweet release of silence. It would soon do the same for his neighbours, and bring the sweet release of death.

### Jolly Ol' Infiltrator

### By

### Weston Kincade

Decorated trees and Christmas memories,

Hours pass with glee.

Families stream down sidewalks,

Small eyes aglitter as they flock,

To see him, the crook,

The jolly elf's shouts taking a page from my book.

I open my luggage—my gift,

An AR-50, my partner this nightshift.

Sitting atop his throne, the chubby thief grins,

"Merry Christmas" resounds—the traitor, my twin.

Smoothing my white beard down, I sight the scope,

Measuring wind and distance, before taking down the Christmas Pope.

At the pull of a trigger, his hat tumbles free,

For there can be only one as jolly as me.

## Shadows

## By

## Antonio Simon, Jr.

Matt rubbed his hands with glee. The room was perfect, which meant at last he'd be safe, though sleep and freedom would be forever out of reach. Fluorescent floodlights in each corner ensured the shadows wouldn't get him. No more reliance on torches or lighters—it was all daylight, all the time.

Then he realized his mistake—more lights didn't mean less shadows, but more of them. Standing in the middle of the room, the four shadows he cast were rooted to his feet. They clapped shut in unison like a Venus flytrap's jaws and pulled him through the floor.

## Winter's Embrace

## By

## Duncan P. Bradshaw

From the corner of my eye, I see her. Behind a skeletal tree, she lurks at the edge of this snow-blanketed forest. Given my tragedy, she must wonder why I've remained. Perhaps she thinks I am still stricken by grief? I skirt around the mounds of the unmarked graves of my family. No insidious chanting from her this day. No poison has she readied for me. Her coven of one will soon be nought but ash. I heft my axe and continue to chop firewood. My revenge is near, and I shall watch her burn atop my wooden pyre.

## Cut Down to Size

### By

## David Owain Hughes

Patrick rolled the cutter from his garage and eyed his overgrown lawn.

"We'll sort it, baby," he said, stroking his lawnmower.

Plugging his Flymo in, Patrick began.

Over the noise, Patrick thought he heard screaming, much like the last time he'd been mowing. Dismissing it, he carried on until he was done and holding a beer.

Whilst admiring his handiwork, the blades of grass started rumbling and moving together like chainsaw teeth. Patrick screamed as his feet burst into clouds of liquid, and he slowly sank into the ground as though he was being fed into a waste disposal unit.

# Children of the Carnival

## By

## Kevin J. Kennedy

I watched them run between the stalls, playing hide and seek. They didn't seem to be bothering with the various rides or confectionary stands. When one of them approached me, and asked if I wanted to play, I looked to my parents. My mother said no, but my father said, "Let the boy be, Janice."

When I found my parents later, they didn't recognise me. I explained that I was their son and I lived with them. They looked at me confused before making their retreat.

The other children and I all play together now, while waiting for another player.

## The Grave

## By

## Amy Cross

You're not fooling me. I know that, despite that great big crack in your face, you're not quite dead yet. You're waiting for me to leave, so you can crawl out of this pit. *Pathetic*. That was always one of your favorite words, wasn't it? Anyway, you should probably close your mouth, unless you want dirt in there. No? Okay, fine. At least I know you're never gonna talk to me like that again. Just know that when I've filled in this grave, I'm going home to figure stuff out. And then? Well, there's one like you in every town.

## Will-o'-the-Wisp

## By

## Nicholas Diak

Deep within the bog, lies a submerged steamboat from a century long since passed. On the clearest of nights, when the cream-coloured moon beams its light through the swamp's canopy, the Will-o'-the-wisp wakens from these old ruins. The wisp dances in the moonlight, her ghostly flames twirl about her, fluttering like the gown she wore during the final dance with her charming beau. On that night, an errant lantern fell, quickly consuming the ship in fire, sinking her and all aboard.

Satisfied with the perfect night, she takes to the marshlands to search for a new partner to dance with.

## Stone

## By

## Becky Narron

The black stone sat in the edge of the water. As my fingers touched it a shock ran up my arm. I pulled my hand away quickly, my face just mere inches from the water.

All of a sudden a thin string shot out and hit me in the face wrapping itself around the back of my head. Then another shot up hitting me between the eyes. I could feel it wiggling it's way inside my flesh.

Several hours later I awoke. I walked in the house and looked in the mirror. My eyes were black. Just like the stone.

## Meal for One

## By

## Howard Carlyle

Charles looked at the raw meat on his plate and slavered like a ravenous dog. He picked it up and tore huge chunks from it with his teeth, eating mouthful after mouthful like it was his last ever meal.

The blood on the flesh was still warm and this just added to the flavor... He couldn't get enough of it. He wiped away the blood from his mouth, looked at the body laid in the corner of the room and thanked her for such a lovely meal.

"You're a pleasure on the eye, and even more so on the tastebuds!"

## Don't Look Back

## By

## James Matthew Buyers

Hush you fool, he's right outside!

He killed both John and Jane!

Rushing in was how they died.

So what? Are you insane?

Silence? What is wrong with you?

That panting sure must suck!

Here's what I think we should do:

We bolt for that old truck.

Grunting? Really? Come on, man!

Is this the time to play?

Hunting us, that is HIS plan!

His ax wants blood today!

Seriously? Now you groan?

My God , are you alright?"

Turning, I see wood and bone;

He swings with all his might.

Ax, skull, crash, flood;

Death, fear, fate, blood ...

I'm next!

## Street-Hearts

## By

## Chris Kelso

Love is here upon my streets: bursting newly infected cells like flimsy water balloons, spewing disease wherever she goes. The girl… she killed this place good and hard. My city. Now, these dead dogs of hope lie stacked in alleyways, and men shake hands as rough as walrus-hide behind the shining shawl of corporate skyscrapers, erected at her behest. Blood whisper softly over asphalt; condom sheaths emerge—ruptured, oozing yellow—from dusty shadows, as if her new parasite has moulted in my filth, shed its hide, and worked its way into the city waterworks. I grow to love her terrorism.

## Consumed by Desire

### By

## Adriaan Brae

My wife woke me with soft kisses. Eager hands slid across my bare chest, pushing blankets aside. She laid her naked body across mine, straddling my hips and we fit blissfully together with the ease of long practice. I stroked up her sides and over her breasts.

Then, her hands gripped my arms, painfully tight. Her lips on mine suddenly vicious. Trapped under her weight, I could only turn my head away—which brought the unmistakable curves of my wife's sleeping body into view. My feeble, choking cries didn't wake her as the succubus began to rip into my flesh.

## Another Tonight?

## By

## William F. Nolan

Night. Cold. Heavy rain. Shining streets.

Blinking neons. Bar. Warm inside. Whiskey Sours. Glow

Ready for another. Feeling strong.

Sexy blonde. Great figure. Alone at bar.

Smiling at him. *Cinch.*

No problem with her. Back at his place.

Her, staggering, holding onto his arm.

Inside apartment. Music on stereo.

Intimate. Cozy. Fire and some wine.

She goes to bathroom. Pills go in her glass.

"Woozy!" she says. "Dizzy."

He smiles. "You'll be fine."

She passes out on sofa.

Knife. Sharp. Uses it. Blood. Lots of it.

Cuts her up. Bags her.

From car to river.

Back to bar.

*Another tonight?*

## Destiny's Embrace

### By

## Michael Paul Gonzalez

Staring down the slavering creature in the corner, Harker knew his destiny had arrived.

He clutched his silver dagger, preparing to pierce the creature's heart, saving the village from eternal damnation.

The bastard-thing had taken his wife, leaving her fang-punctured heart on his table, next to his daughter's eyes.

Tonight, he swore, it would end.

Harker knew this was the moment when heroes were forged, legends born.

As he tripped over his own feet,
and stumbled into the creature's icy embrace, he realized he was no hero.
The creature's jaws snapped through his throat, drowning his final scream in blood.

## Clean

### By

### Valerie Lioudis

No matter how many times I wash my hands, the red just won't disappear. Well, not red really, but more of a crimson. His blood. My blood. Who knew where one ended and the other began? He put up a good fight, and that made me grateful. Each swing feeds the beast inside me and may keep him at bay for a bit. He had the upper hand for a moment, and the beast roared. For a second, I wished he would end me. Red bubbles swirl clockwise down the drain as the beast spins to nest in my mind.

## Trees

## By

## Donelle Pardee Whiting

"The trees, Mama!" I cried.

"What about them?"

"They wanna get me."

Sighing, Mama glanced up from pruning roses. "It's just your imagination. You really need to stop making up stories."

While she looked, the trees appeared normal—a bit overgrown, with a few branches draped over the backyard wall.

"Mama, look. They're climbing over the wall."

When she didn't answer, I peeked at the garden. But she was gone. One shoe lay in the flowers.

I looked at the wall again. One tree turned as if to look at me, and pointed with one spindly, leaf-covered branch.

*They're here.*

# Dancing

## By

## David Owain Hughes

"Girls, stop arguing and biting each other!"

"Bitch drew blood, Dougie."

"I don't care. Get on that *fucking* stage, Dallas." The fat boss snapped his fingers. "Time's money."

Dallas stumbled through the beaded entryway, collapsing against the runway's pole. She felt sick, but managed to gyrate her semi-naked body. Music played.

"Over here, baby!" a guy called, waving a fistful of singles.

She sauntered towards him, hair covering her face.

"Get 'em titties—"

She flew at him with vacant eyes, mouth open. Her teeth latched onto his throat, and she ripped his jugular apart, drinking the hot, squirting blood.

## Running from Him

## By

## Michael A. Arnzen

Kite string spools and Charlie knows he's finally caught a good gust, so he turns and charges down the beach as fast as he can, enjoying the resistance, the tension tugging, his feet kicking sand. He remembers the time his big brother once chased him with an axe, so now he runs faster, even faster, and he doesn't stop until he finally runs out of string and turns, breathless, to look up in the sky....

The flesh kite swivels in sunbeams, tiny as a bat.

A drop of bloody sweat lands on his forehead.

Charlie chuckles and wipes. "Ewww, bro."

## Night Terrors

## By

## Lisa Vasquez

The curious circumstance of his absence was detailed in black ink across headlines. He gazed out from behind a pinhole of light created by the keyhole in the darkness.

"Tell us again, ma'am?" the officer asked, with a mixture of compassion and suspicion.

"I tucked him in last night, then heard him scream. When I ran in he was gone, and the closet was empty."

She pointed toward the door, and the officer looked at it. They had already checked it.

"I... keep hearing scratches from inside," his mother sobbed.

The hair on his arm raised as childhood fears resurfaced.

## It's Just a Dream, Right?

### By

### Ellen A. Easton

For as long as I can remember, it was always the same. Terrified to go to sleep, but unwilling to wake up, no matter how much I wanted to. It was different this time. Same bloody nightmare, filled with death and dismemberment.

But it seemed real. I could feel the bones snapping, hear the wet squelching of muscles torn apart. The acrid bitterness of bile and blood filled my nose. I looked down, hands darkened and dripping. My hands.

I woke up screaming. Sitting up, I turned on my lamp and sighed, until my shadow turned to me and lunged.

## Over the Edge

## By

## Mark Cassell

Adrian lives alone and doesn't have any children, yet the sound of giggling snatches him from sleep. Moonlight reveals stickfigures scrawled across the wall. With one foot tangled in sheets, the other hanging over the edge, he jerks upright.

Something scratches, just out of sight – pencils? He twists and squints.

More stick-figures, even now being drawn, only this time, given attention by red detail, stark beneath the moon's glow.

Sweat prickles his forehead.

More sketching, more red detail…

Agony spears up his leg, from his dangling foot.

A pencil juts from his ankle. Blood gushes, warm - just like the stick-figures.

## The Beauty of the Sea

### By

### Kevin J. Kennedy

A caravan by the sea had seemed like a great idea, until the creatures crawled out of the water. They were the size of large dogs, but clearly a strange combination of lobsters and crabs. The weird hybrid had somehow mutated. They swarmed the caravan site, shredding anyone in their path, their pincers cutting through metal as if it was butter. Sitting on top of the caravan, I hoped they would pass us by after they killed everyone in the open, but it's as if they can smell us. We are surrounded now. The sea doesn't look as beautiful anymore.

# Breadth of Bone

## By

## Sara Tantlinger

"*Misery*. Mis-er-ee," she repeated, as if fascinated by how the letters felt. Her peachy mouth captured the word perfectly. "It's all in the lips," she told him. "No tongue."

His hands shook. "I know." The blade pressed against her back in that way she liked. She paid him little mind and watched her own pursing lips in the mirror. Sunlight glittered through the window, casting a multihued gleam onto the knife.

"Just a little deeper than last time," she said. Always, *just a little deeper*.

He speared her *just a little deeper*, losing track of when moans turned to screams.

## Never Leave Me, Nor Forsake Me

### By

### Mike Duke

Wrists and ankles shackled to the gurney, leather straps secure forehead and chin. Polished, stainless steel utensils rest on sterile blue fabric. Wide eyes, held open by a mechanical device stare up at a surgeon's mask. Pupils, plump with terror just moments before, now shrink away from bright operating room lights.

Yet, icepick and hammer in hand, he sees only love.

"Don't worry. When you wake up, you'll feel right as rain. You'll never, ever want to leave me again."

Warm smile. Cold kiss on her skin. Icepick touches corner of eye. Hammer rises... and a content wife is born.

# Escape

## By

## Megan Ince

Every fiber in her body was screaming to stop, but the screeches and noises behind her in the dark forest kept her legs moving.

The forest was starting to thin out. There was a reason no one went into the forest. Pale, nasty, crawling things had shredded her friends before her eyes. She was barely able to slip away.

Her legs finally slowed down as she started to cry. She wanted to keep running, but the ground stopped. Staring over the cliff edge, she was suddenly calm. One final step.

The rush of wind finally drowned out the horrible creatures.

## Forever Men

## By

## Eric J. Guignard

They're odd men, should you glimpse them, those three brothers living in the veiled moors of Lower Thorncombe--gaunt and grim and old, their skin wan from sleeping in the day, their eyes filled with tales from long ago. Some call 'em Brothers Death, but those of us who have been here long enough--who have peered toward that horizon which has no dawn, o'er the vast sea without tide, or have even touched the cold of its bleak shallows--we know them as Forever Men, for they carry off the unfortunates who wade into that lightless Sea of Oblivion.

# The Artist

## By

## Howard Carlyle

Now stripped, their skins were tossed to one side and their corpses were all neatly hung in a line, on hooks, along the wall. Each corpse varied in size, both male and female. He stood back to admire his work. He saw himself as an artist with a finished masterpiece, there in the flesh… or, actually, minus their flesh.

Before skillfully skinning them , he saw them as a blank canvas, but now they were perfect… a perfect piece of art of his own creating. It wasn't their outside appearance that interested him.

After all, beauty is on the inside.

# Initiation

## By

## Mark Fleming

I'm at the cliff's edge. I know the gang will be watching. They're always there, spying. Their voices threaten constantly. But this is all I have to do to be accepted, to join them: this quick initiation. Heart hammering, I kick my trainers aside. Several deep breaths, then I dive. For seconds I'm flying through the void.... into a black wall. Through the churning waters I imagine the screams of everyone who has jumped before me, hear their splintering bones. Lungs expiring, I fight towards the surface. No one will be waiting to cheer. I think I've always known.

## What's For Dinner?

## By

## Christopher Motz

Bernie had never been a fan of his grandmother, but her holiday dinners were epic.

This year was like all others, except for the fact that the house smelled more like roadkill than savory, baked turkey.

The table was set, but in the place of steaming trays of meat and corn were piles of writhing maggots and dusty plates.

Bernie saw Grandma seconds later, dangling from a rope in front of the dry Christmas tree.

A three sentence note was pinned to her sagging flesh.

*Make your own fucking dinner.*

*Your grandfather is hanging in the garage.*

*Merry Christmas, assholes!*

# Vermillion

## By

## Lisa Vasquez

A film of dreamy, winter white covered her eyes as she awoke. Ringing in her ears muted the screams of those around her, their blurry faces like masks of fear as they mouthed words she could not hear.

*Where am I?* she thought to herself, trying to make sense of the chaos. Her vision cleared. She saw the white walls painted with splashes of red, and bodies on the floor stared back at her through cold, lifeless eyes. The memory came flooding back, as the priest pressed the crucifix to her brow, "See the cross of the Lord, hostile thing!"

# Jack Frost

## By

## Christina Bergling

His icy finger traced freezing lines along my skin. The bitter spires penetrated deep through my flesh, piercing down to my unsuspecting bones. The frost branched out, seizing my cells, captivating them. I felt my body constrict as my own skin enclosed me tighter. When I exhaled, a curling plume floated up from my lips. Yet each breath became smaller, slower. The world itself became lethargic and heavy. I felt the weight on my eyes as I struggled to move. As the ice spread into my brain, darkness closed like a waning vignette around my mind, until all thought ceased.

## Coming Around

### By

### C.M. Saunders

He was being chased down a long, dark tunnel by a pack of dogs. He couldn't see them, but he could hear them panting and snarling. They were gaining on him.

His chest burned. Couldn't catch his breath. Shooting pains.

Then the tunnel and the dogs began to melt away, and Duncan's world was spinning into focus. That was a dream?

Where the fuck was he?

Then he remembered: the operation, heart surgery.

He tried to open his eyes, but couldn't. Too soon.

But he could hear noises, like someone tuning a radio. Voices.

"Too bad we couldn't save him."

## Bad Cop, Bad Cop

## By

## James H Longmore

104 degrees of Texas heat, the corpulent cop has my keys; he's been in my car since he clocked me going five miles over the speed limit, showing me clips of *vee-hicular accidents*- odd how people are still alive when he gets to them...

The stifling air reeks of sweat and the underlying stench of *something*- is it possible to smell *crazy*?

Gwendolyn adds to the stink with her shit-filled diaper, fine blonde hair plastered to her sweat-drenched scalp, fontanel pulsing slowly as she fights to breathe.

Desperate, my hand reaches the door.

"Ma'am..." the cop grasps his gun.

## Experimental Animal 7

### By

### Lee McGeorge

Soldiers on snowmobiles. High speed under moonlight. The convoy halts and the prisoner is pushed out.

"Start running," a soldier says.

Prisoner runs like hell in deep snow.

Tracked vehicle with a cargo container opens up. Experimental Animal 7 crawls out. The body of a leopard, the long snout of a wolf, bigger than a family car. Screams and blood, it shreds the prisoner in seconds.

The animal turns to the soldiers, snarling, blood on its snout. Still hungry. Leaps on the closest man. Gunfire. Panic. Limbs torn off. Shooting ends with a final howl.

Escaped.

Last seen heading West.

## Bummed Light

## By

## James Matthew Byers

"Has anybody got a light?"

He asked to no avail.

About the body, bound and tight,

The keeners let a wail.

A cigarette between his lips

Remained within a dance

As if it moved, Hawaiian hips,

A secretive romance-

Around it turned as others cried,

Awaiting fiery sorts.

Investigating who had died,

He puffed at his reports.

So certain that this was the place

Until the mourning came,

The questions etching out his face

Revealed a banshee's game

As, all at once, the cigarette

Lit up and made him choke,

And suddenly to his regret,

He drowned within its smoke.

## Sugar & Spice

## By

## Chad Lutzke

The tickle in his ear had been there for days. It scratched and scraped and clicked like a playing card in the spokes of a bicycle.

"Abby, what have you done?"

The man's daughter sat beside him, a grin on her face.

"When I asked Mommy for a puppy she said to put a bug in your ear."

"Honey, it's only an expression."

The man could hear the distant groan of his wife, her agony growing louder, closer.

"Abby, what did you do to Mommy?"

"Nothing, Daddy." The girl's grin remained.

"Mommy said she'd keep an eye out for one."

# Air

## By

## Dave McClusky

The cold encompassed him. His lungs burnt in their desire to fulfil their natural function—to breathe!

His eyes were wide, yet his vision was shaky. Obscure shapes around him attempted to hit him with objects. Each of them, ultimately missing.

He wanted to scream. He needed to open his mouth and allow the sweet, life-giving air rush into him, easing the fire in his chest.

That way lay death, but that was inevitable now.

Inside the cabinet the escape-artist opened his mouth. Cold water rushed in, filling his lungs, as the audience tried in vain to smash the glass.

## You Don't See Me

## By

## Christina Bergling

You don't see me. You come home to the house you assume is empty.

You don't see me. You walk around your house in your underwear, dancing to the music vibrating the speaker.

You don't see me. You cook dinner for one and dribble noodles onto your lap in front of the television.

You don't see me. You lock us in together and turn out all the lights.

You don't see me. You pull the covers up tight and start to breathe slow and heavy.

You don't see me. I climb in bed with you and squeeze out your life.

# The Dead Train

## By

## Craig Saunders

A red-rusted, warped relic, the dead train clacks through tunnels - a revenant's bone feet staggering on cold stone.

A man, a shade in the darkness, sideways of time, waits.

The ghost train rolls in. Doors slide aside and he steps aboard.

A woman, the other side of time, steps toward doors which are not there.

Wind fills the tunnel before commuters cry out at the blood. Flesh and bone speckle silent tracks beneath a carriage.

The waiting shade takes her hand and they wait for others. There are always those who rush to meet the dead train too early.

## Delivery

## By

## Briana Robertson

Water gushed between her legs, soaking the tattered edges of her filthy nightgown. Panic's frigid chill raced down her spine.

"Oh, God. Help me! Please!"

Her already ragged nails ripped to the quick as she clawed at the locked door.

She collapsed as the spasms took control. Harder. Faster. Blind in the Cimmerian basement, her nostrils swamped with the cloying scent of mildew, she curled in on herself, cursing her captor.

Pain peaked. Breath quickened. Her heartbeat stuttered and slowed.

The baby slid free, silent, limp, and cold.

She answered Death's call ...

Her son's piteous cry came too late.

## The Guest

## By

## Dave McCluskey

Outside, the wind howled, chilling me to the core. An innocuous sound, but what it heralded petrified me.

A figure peered in from outside. Its ancient eyes dismissing me; it knew what it wanted.

A whisper, somehow louder than the storm outside, announced its entrance as ice cold tendrils pierced my heart...

'I knew you'd come,' I croaked.

Ignoring me, its eyes sought out its goal.

The body lying on the table elevated at my guest's instruction. My beautiful baby floated towards the thing with the eternal eyes.

Then they were gone, taking the storm, and my heart, with them!

## Nights in Whitechapel

### By

### Theresa Jacobs.

"Ambiguous!" Phlegm rattles in his throat as he scoffs, "I'll show them!" Jack steps back to admire his handy work.

The message is clear in his mind, as he leaves two fleshy mounds on the nightstand.

The whore's blood already coagulating on his thin, black, leather gloves. Though he feels he has much more to do, time is a foe. Grabbing up his cane, Jack slips from the lodging room and melds with the London fog.

Until, a few minutes later, he spots Mary Kelly. A solitary figure in the dead of night, and he, with a message to send.

# Betrayal

## By

# Lee Mountford

My heart is broken.

Sarah, the love of my life, flaunts around before my eyes. She is on the phone, arranging a date for this very evening.

At *our* house.

She giggles and flirts, caring not for me or for our relationship.

I see now that my feelings for her are unrequited. All the times I kept her safe from the *wrong* kind of man was for nothing.

Well, I will not stand for this betrayal. No more hiding in the attic, watching and waiting. Now it is time to reveal myself to her.

And to cut out her heart.

## Beautiful Francesca

## By

## Ike Hamill

I've adored her for sixty-eight days. Ever since I was fired, Francesca is my job. She hums to herself in the morning when she brushes her hair. The TV in the living room is always on—I guess so she doesn't feel so alone. Deadbolts and window latches are a social contract. They're not really stopping anyone. She is so beautiful. I long to see loving gratitude in her eyes as I carry her to safety, rescuing her from danger.

But she is never in danger.

Francesca is always in control.

First, I'll have to put her in danger.

## Priscilla's Pugnacious Pampered Pups

## By

## Brandy Yassa

Customary 'cuppa' consumed, liberally spiked, Priscilla Pempley prepared for sleep.

On the TV, in the background for ambience, she woozily noticed the end of a close-captioned message; something about "an unknown source", and warning viewers to be cautious.

Clucking her tongue dismissively, she settled in with her three pampered Pomeranian pooches.

She awoke suddenly, the air smelling odd, and feeling watched. Lifting her eye mask, she startled, finding her dogs staring at her. Chuckling, she began smiling, until, as one, they all commenced snarling.

"Wha...", she started, then screamed, as her once faithful furry friends tore her throat out.

## Mister Fancy Pants

## By

## Rhys Hughes

I'm walking home from the theater one evening.

"Mister Fancy Pants!" The heckler a youth sitting on a wall. He swings his legs and repeats his scornful call, "Mister Fancy Pants!" and the colour drains from my cheeks.

I no longer stride confidently, but stumble.

Shame has made me awkward.

I reach my house and remove my trousers with the alacrity of a humiliated acrobat. . There in the hallway mirror I see myself and my original underpants, made from ripe avocado skins, stitched together with golden thread and studded with opals and pearls.

"How did he know?" I mutter, distraught.

## Greed Has No Heart

## By

## Mark Lumby

It rattled the open drawer like a tribal drum. I floated to my feet, cold and light, from where I sat. I moved to the drawer, not thinking why I couldn't feel the heat from the open fire. I ignored this, followed the noise. The drum stopped. Inside the drawer, the organ struggled to pump absent blood. I felt obliged to turn... the cavity in my chest that once accommodated a heart, now home to stained money. Money was stuffed in my mouth, too. I heard a door close, the killer leave.

'Greed has no heart' was written in blood.

## Beast in the Bedroom

### By

### Pippa Bailey

Her bed creaked, or was it the wind outside? Faye didn't like noises that invaded her home at night. This was different. A scratching, grinding sound, like nails on a chalk board. She screwed her eyes tight, and wished them away. Thud!. The window flew open. Cold night air whipped the covers from her naked body, swiftly followed by a gigantic, hairy fist that tore her from the bed. She clawed at the mattress, but it yanked her free and out of the window. Face to face with a gigantic beast, it stole her away into the inky blackness.

## The Boy

## By

## Richard Chizmar and Billy Chizmar

The boy emerged from his hole after thirty-nine days. He had finally run out of water. The sky was the color of a nasty bruise he'd gotten last summer after falling off his skateboard. Black, purple, red - It was an angry sky. The boy didn't know if it was day or night. Ash fell like snow flurries. It was a grey world now. *They* had burned everything. He started for the blasted skeleton of a nearby house when he felt *their* heat on the back of his neck. The boy turned to face *them*, but all he saw was fire.

## Weeping Keys

## By

## Elizabeth Cash

There are eighty-eight keys on a piano:

fifty-two white and thirty-six black.

Each key played sounds a different note, as do the people who lay before me.

Each ligament that is torn and each muscle that is cut offers a new sound to fall from their quivering lips.

Some say it's cynical, I say it's methodical.

But what they don't understand is, that I'm doing them a justice - a peace. Taking their life to give another.

They don't deserve to breed. They don't even deserve to feel the pain which I have so graciously given them.

Let them weep.

## Grand Slam

## By

## Christina Bergling

She dragged the wooden bat slowly along the concrete. I could hear the tiny splinters firing away from the friction. *Scrape, SLAM!* She taunted me, moving around me. I flinched and clutched my aching ribs as she paced.

"I hope he was worth it," she laughed.

I did not bother to speak; words had earned her batting a grand slam against my ribcage. *Scrape, SLAM!* Closer this time. I felt my heartbeat climb into my ears. The fear blotted out my thoughts.

She lifted the bat, casting a shadow over me. The impact shattered the world before it went black.

## Shock Collar

## By

## Jeff Strand

"It's no big deal," said the man. "You just can't go more than 100 yards from the invisible fence. Step outside that boundary and you get zapped. Remain outside of it and the shocks continue until you step back in. Simple."

"Please don't do this," said Jerry, tugging at the tight collar around his neck. "I apologized. What more can I do?"

The man smiled. "You can stay within the boundary so you don't get third degree burns on your neck."

"Please!"

"Stop begging." The man signaled to the driver, and the truck with the equipment sped off. "Start running."

## The Festival of Gluttony

## By

## Mike Duke

First snow.

The Hibernation is upon us again and The Festival of Gluttony; to gorge ourselves, then sleep...together in the hidden caves.

I help Mother with the preparations.

The men load muskets and sharpen blades for The Hunt; hitch the covered wagon to Clydesdales. Thick beams of wood, with deep sides designed for heavy loads; easily fifty human corpses. More if the number of children is high.

Which is always nice. They *are* the most tender.

The cold keeps the meat from turning on their way home. When they arrive, my duties begin.

I'm the best skinner.

Momma says so.

## Selfie

## By

## Rick Gualtieri

It was nothing, so silly, just playing around with my new phone in the bathroom. Took a selfie of myself and posted it online. Not a big deal, until it was. Friends pointed it out, thinking I faked it, but I didn't. I'm as surprised as they are – surprised, but frightened, too.

Behind me, in the mirror, stands my reflection, but it's not right. It's facing the camera and staring at me, a mix of hatred and loathing in its eyes. How long has it pretended to be me? And, now that I know, how long before it stops pretending?

# Jonathan

## By

## Amy Cross

The last time I saw him was on the Old Kent Road. He was dressed in his finest Sunday clothes, as if he was on his way to the club. He looked magnificent, although no-one else seemed to notice him. He didn't see me – perhaps he *couldn't* see me – but I watched as he slipped quietly through the crowd. I wondered how much he remembered of that fateful day six months earlier. Certainly he seemed to be smiling, but he was limping badly and he seemed not to have picked any of the glass out of his face.

## A Flash Beginning

## By

## Jessica Gomez

The new world's a nightmare come to life, stripping luxuries and normalities; confiscating all hopes and dreams of a future with family and friends. Tears stream down my soot-covered face, leaving salty trails in their wake.

Screams fill the air, like the smoke billowing off the city around us. A quiet growl sounds from the bundle in my arms, bringing me back to my reality. My heart shatters, devastated, as a sob escapes.

There's only one option remaining.

I cuddle her close, placing my baby's mouth next to my neck, and wait for the bite.

Where she goes, I go.

## Spellbound

## By

## John Dover

I wave my hands and the air crackles to life. I concocted the brew, I spoke the words. The sting from the cut on my hand'll wane. The sour tang of sick, fighting its way out will pass with the wave of adrenaline. These minor discomforts are worth the enslavement of the beast.

They'll all pay. It'll flay them alive and bring me their hearts as gifts.

I'm sure it won't matter that the words on the page bleed together. I incanted a viable enough facsimile. I'm sure it's licking my neck out of honor and not sampling its meal.

## I Was a Teenage Eulogist

### By

### Jason M. Light

I was a teenage eulogist.

When I was fifteen, I found an old typewriter and eulogized the little old lady next door. She died the next day. I wrote more, for goldfish and dogs and cats. I wrote them for friends, neighbors, and strangers. They all died the next day.

I still write them, I don't know why - I can't help it. I don't do it on purpose; I'm no murderer.

I've been working all day and night. The midnight hour is nigh. It might be a black hole or gamma rays. War is imminent.

I was a teenage eulogist.

## From the Mouths of Drunks and Babes

## By

## Alex Laybourne

"Aliens," they cried, running panicked through the streets.

Nobody believed them. They were drunk, one heavy set man with a beard was wearing a pair of bunny ears, for crying out loud.

"Aliens, aliens are coming." One of their group stopped right by us, grabbing me by the shirt, the stench of tequila strong on his breath.

I pushed him away and he promptly threw up over his shoes before running after his screaming friends.

We laughed at them, drunken fools. Looking back, I guess the laugh is on us now. Those of us that are still alive at least.

## Stage Fright

## By

## James McCulloch

The putrid stench burned his nostrils as he dragged the body across the floor. He had heard the smell of the dead was overpowering, but nothing could have prepared him for this.

The stage lights came on, hitting him like a punch to the face. He had been warned not to look at the audience, their excited chattering adding to the assault on his senses. He walked away as the chattering made way for the crunching of bone—filling their gullets with the poor soul he'd left behind.

He just wanted to be away before the poor bastard woke up.

# Cupid and Death

## By

## Rhys Hughes

Cupid and Death exchanged arrows.

Death prefers the scythe to the bow, but Cupid isn't brawny enough to swing an implement of such awkward mass.

They parted and went their separate ways, but by chance they fired at the same individual at the same instant.

One arrow in his chest, one in his back.

As the arrows hit, the man fell in love with Death. But love was killed inside him. The arrows met in his middle and death fell in love with love, but love was killed by death, its lover.

How could death not kill itself after that?

## The Feast

## By

## Rebecca Brae

They call me Lady Raven—or Witch, depending on how superstitious they are. I've fed my lovelies for years. The tree in my backyard is a living fortress of Stygian beaks and wings. One sits on my chest, staring. All I can do is glare back.

I fell while hanging their feeder and landed badly. He caws an invitation to his family. I feel nothing as they tug at my exposed belly. How long until my husband comes home? Blood sprays. Oh gods, they've pulled something out; something I don't want to see. How long will I have to watch?

## The Dolls

## By

## Mark Lukens

"Mom, when are we leaving?"

"As soon as your father fixes the engine. Why don't you play with your dolls?"

"I'm saving them for later. I had to hide them in a box."

"From your sister?"

"Yes. She already broke all of her dolls. She pulled their arms and legs off. She smashed their heads flat and stomped on them."

"She shouldn't do that."

"She's always mean to her dolls."

"It's a waste. We're not getting any more dolls on this trip."

"Mom?"

"Yes?"

"What do the dolls call themselves down there on their own planet?"

"They call themselves humans."

## Afterword

I always feel that every book takes you on a journey, with anthologies often taking you on several. The stories in this book are extremely short, but I think all of the authors involved packed a lot into them. I hope you enjoyed our anthology of drabbles and, if you are new to flash fiction, I hope we have made a convert of you. This is the first collection I've worked on where almost all of the authors messaged me to tell me how much fun they had writing their stories. I think it shines through in these drabbles.

Putting this book together allowed me to work with more authors than I would have ever had a chance to with a normal anthology. A lot of the authors in this book have appeared in my previous anthologies and the rest I worked with me for the first time. It was a pleasure working with each and every one of them. When I decide to do one of these books, I often try to talk myself out of it due to the amount of work involved, but it's also a guilty pleasure, as I have authors that I have been reading for the last twenty years sending me stories to read. I've said a few times that I'm not going to do another anthology, but by now I've realised that I don't think I can stop.

Normally at the end of a book like this, you would find a list of the contributing authors and links to their websites. Most of the authors in this book have a personal bio that is much longer than the drabble they have written. For that reason there is no 'Author Bio' section. I just don't think it makes sense to have an author bio section that's longer than the story content. Almost every author has a Facebook and Twitter account and many have websites that you can find easily if you search online. I encourage you to check them out, they have a wealth of great work among them.

# Also available on Amazon from KJK Publishing

# Kevin J. Kennedy Presents

| C.S. Anderson | Rick Gualtieri | Lisa Morton |
| Michael A. Arnzen | Kevin J. Kennedy | Steven Murray |
| Christina Bergling | Weston Kincade | Willow Rose |
| Amy Cross | Andrew Lennon | Ty Schwamberger |
| Tim Curran | J.L. Lane | Veronica Smith |
| Israel Finn | John R. Little | Lisa Vasquez |
| Suzanne Fox | Xtina Marie | Peter Oliver Wonder |
| Rose Garnett | J.C. Michael | |

Foreword by Nev Murray   Edited by Brandy Yassa

# COLLECTED CHRISTMAS

## HORROR SHORTS

## KEVIN J KENNEDY PRESENTS

C.S. Anderson
Christina Bergling
James Matthew Byers
Mark Cassell
David Chrisley
Amy Cross
Mark Fleming
Latashia Figueroa

Suzanne Fox
Lex Jones
Kevin J. Kennedy
Weston Kincade
Andrew Lennon
Mark Lukens
Jeff Menapace
JC Michael

Christopher Motz
Briana Robertson
Veronica Smith
Steven Stacy
Jeff Strand
Lisa Vasquez
Peter Oliver Wonder

Foreword by Nev Murray

Edited by Brandy Yassa

# COLLECTED EASTER HORROR SHORTS

KEVIN J. KENNEDY PRESENTS
COLLECTED
HALLOWEEN
HORROR SHORTS

# YOU ONLY GET ONE SHOT

**KEVIN J. KENNEDY**
**J.C. MICHAEL**

*"Gleefully disturbing and darkly terrifying to writers like me, this is such a clever and diffuse story, with the same puzzling torment of the SAW movies."*

Michael A. Arnzen, Bram Stoker Award winning author of *Play Dead*

Printed in Poland
by Amazon Fulfillment
Poland Sp. z o.o., Wrocław